To Jan and Robin and Katie,

This book has pictures of your friends Madeleine and Paddy in and what's more, pictures of Macarthur Square in Carlton. Just up the road from where Jan and I used to live.

Best wishes

Rachel [illegible]

BRIDGIT WAS BORED

ANN MOORHEAD and PETER HILLARY

Illustrated by RACHEL TONKIN

Hodder & Stoughton

SYDNEY AUCKLAND LONDON TORONTO

For Amelia Rose and George
and
for Madeleine and Isabel

First published in 1992
by Hodder & Stoughton (Australia) Pty Limited
ACN 000 884 855
10-16 South Street, Rydalmere NSW 2116

Hillary, Peter.
Bridgit was bored.

ISBN 0 340 57844 0

I. Moorhead, Ann. II. Tonkin, Rachel. III. Title.

823.914

Typeset by G.T. Setters, Sydney.
Printed in Hong Kong by Colorcraft.

Bored, bored, bored!

Bridgit was unquestionably bored. Yes, she thought, "I am completely bored."

Bridgit lived in a tall and narrow house that looked out on to a narrow square.

Today she sat on the floor in her bedroom with the shutters closed. "Outside is boring and inside is boring too," she thought to herself.

Bridgit's mother and father looked into the bedroom. "What's wrong?" they asked.

"The houses are grey, the cars are dirty, the leaves are falling off the trees, there's nothing to do and there's no-one to play with," Bridgit said.

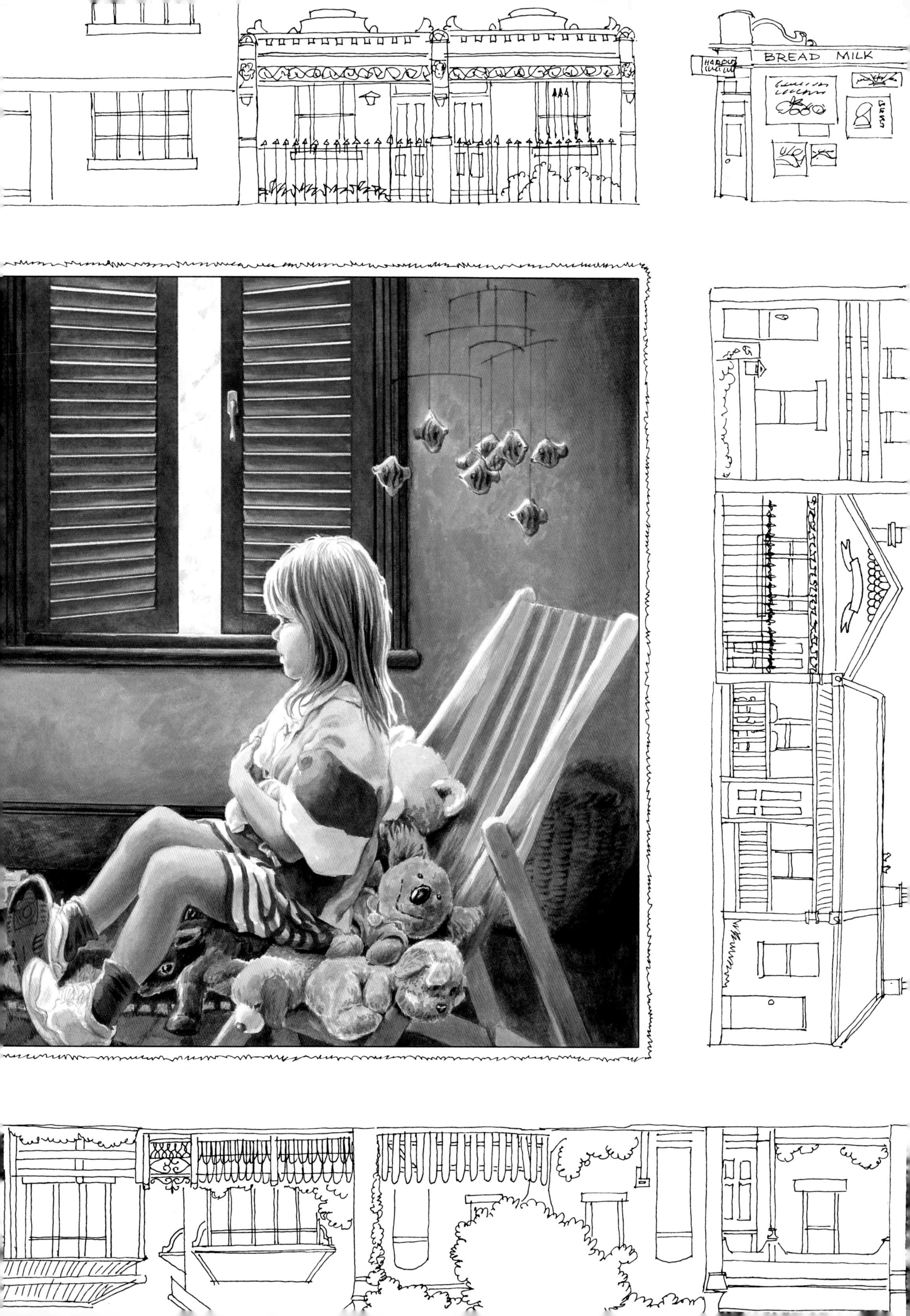
BREAD MILK

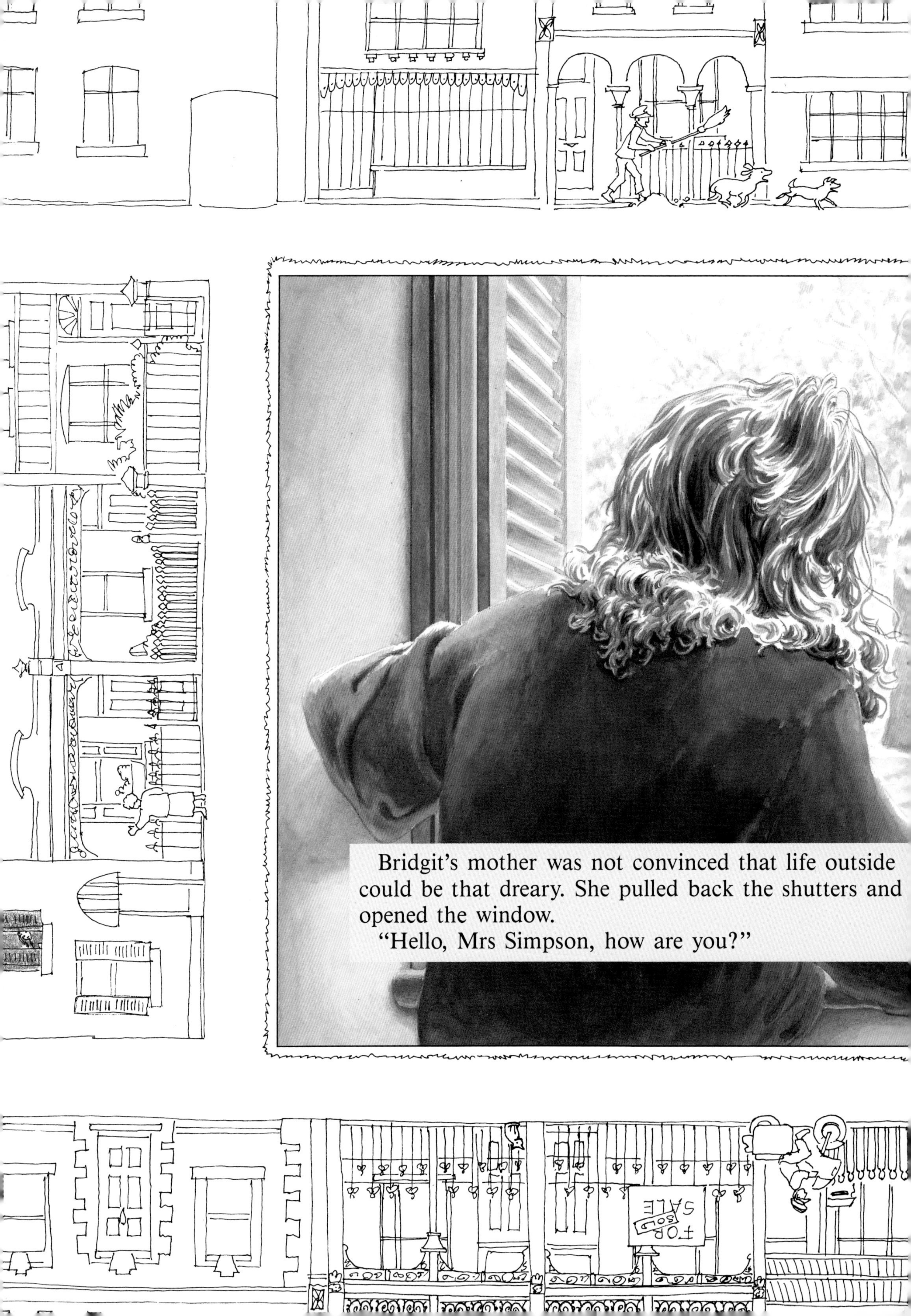

Bridgit's mother was not convinced that life outside could be that dreary. She pulled back the shutters and opened the window.

"Hello, Mrs Simpson, how are you?"

BREAD MILK

FOR SALE
SOLD

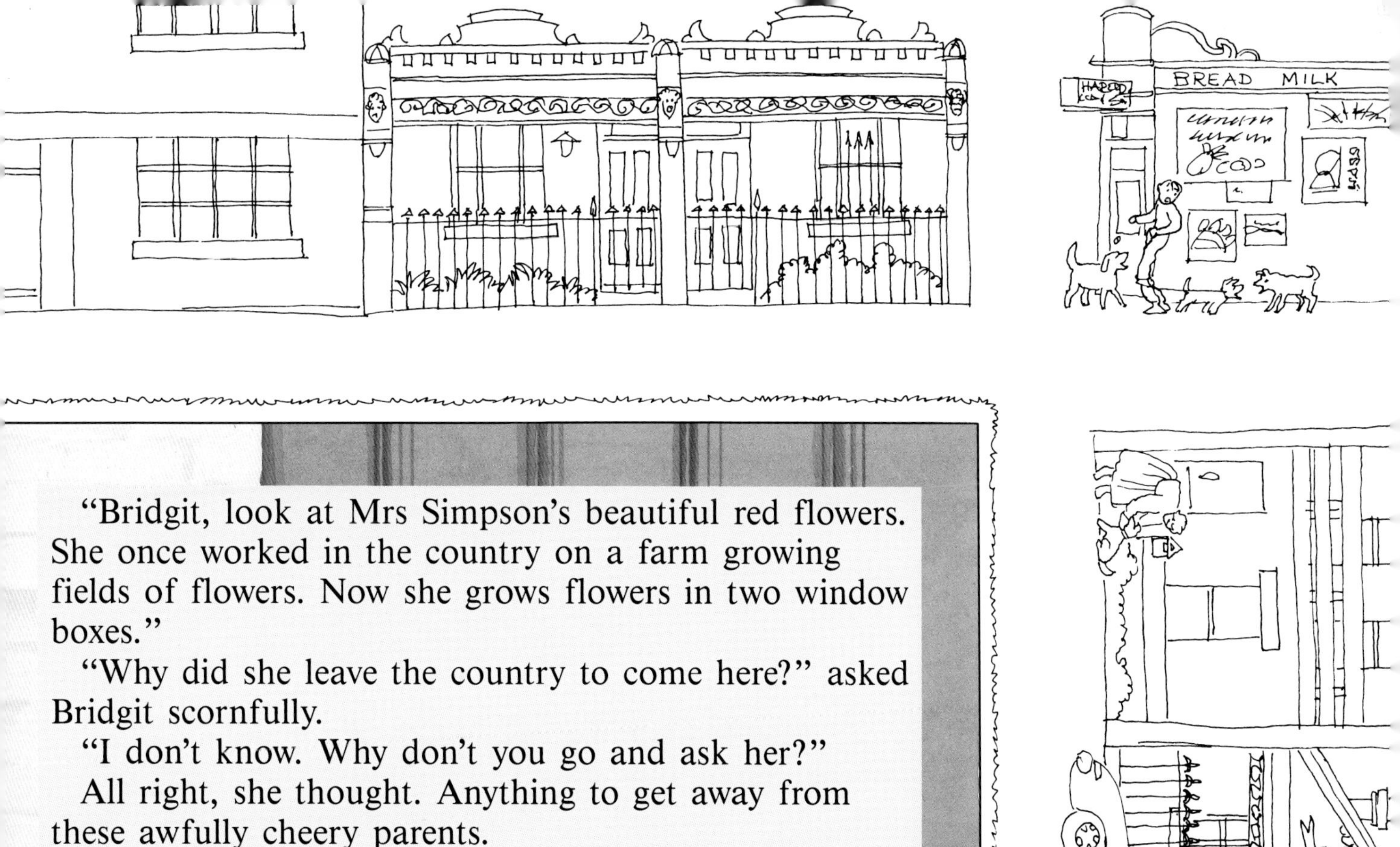

"Bridgit, look at Mrs Simpson's beautiful red flowers. She once worked in the country on a farm growing fields of flowers. Now she grows flowers in two window boxes."

"Why did she leave the country to come here?" asked Bridgit scornfully.

"I don't know. Why don't you go and ask her?"

All right, she thought. Anything to get away from these awfully cheery parents.

Mrs Simpson smiled. "I am far too old to work on the land." She handed Bridgit a bright red flower. "Now I live here and can go to the cafes, go shopping for delectable chocolates and visit the zoo whenever I want to. . .haw haw. Naughty me!"

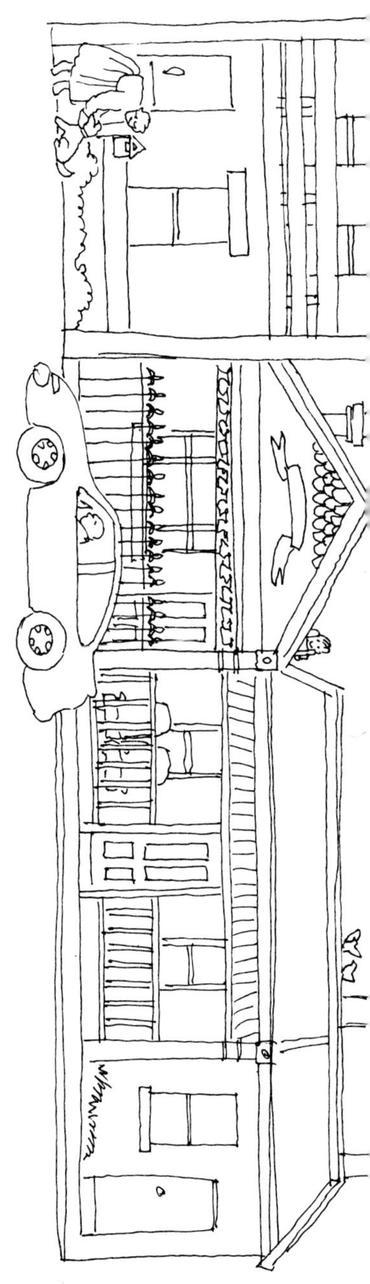

Bridgit waved and walked on. She knew her parents were watching her.

Next door to Mrs Simpson's house is Mr Chuan's house which has a broad veranda where he likes to sit on his day off. Today Mr Chuan was wearing his tram driver's uniform and was on his way to work. Whenever he sees Bridgit he always asks, "What are you going to do today, Bridgit?"

"Good morning, Mr Chuan," Bridgit said.

"Oh, hello. What are you going to do today, Bridgit?"

Mr Lucas was outside his house sweeping up the leaves which he does three times a day during the autumn. He hates leaves and usually looks annoyed while he sweeps the red and gold leaves into neat piles.

"Hi, Mr Lucas," Bridgit called, stepping carefully between the piles of leaves.

"Arrr. . ., Bridgit. A perfect windless day for raking up leaves. Couldn't be better for the job."

Bridgit notices a large van speeding up the street. Uh-oh! She knew what would happen next.

BREAD MILK

Leaves are Lovely
Plant delivery service.
Leaves
Lovely
Plant

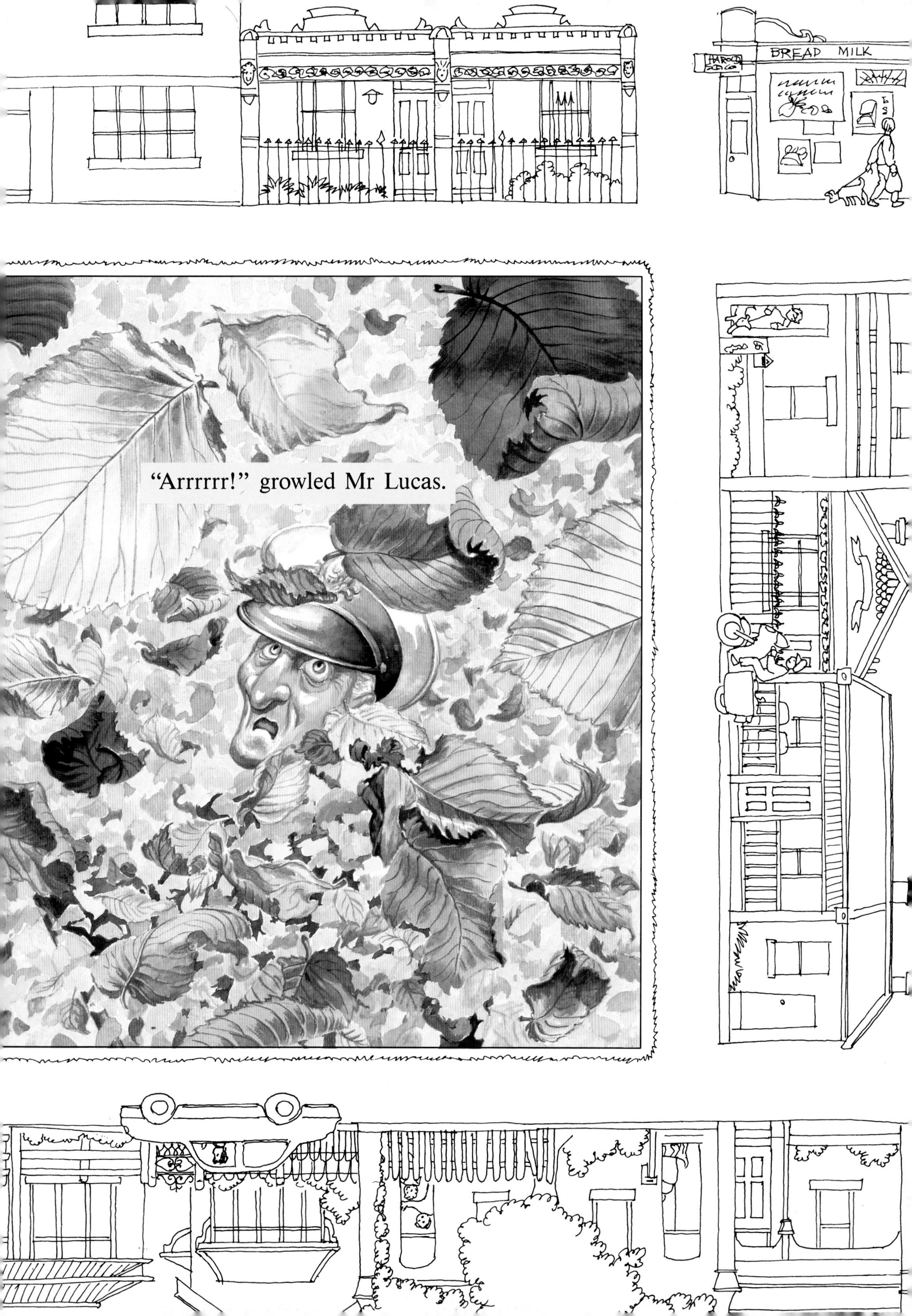
BREAD MILK
"Arrrrrr!" growled Mr Lucas.

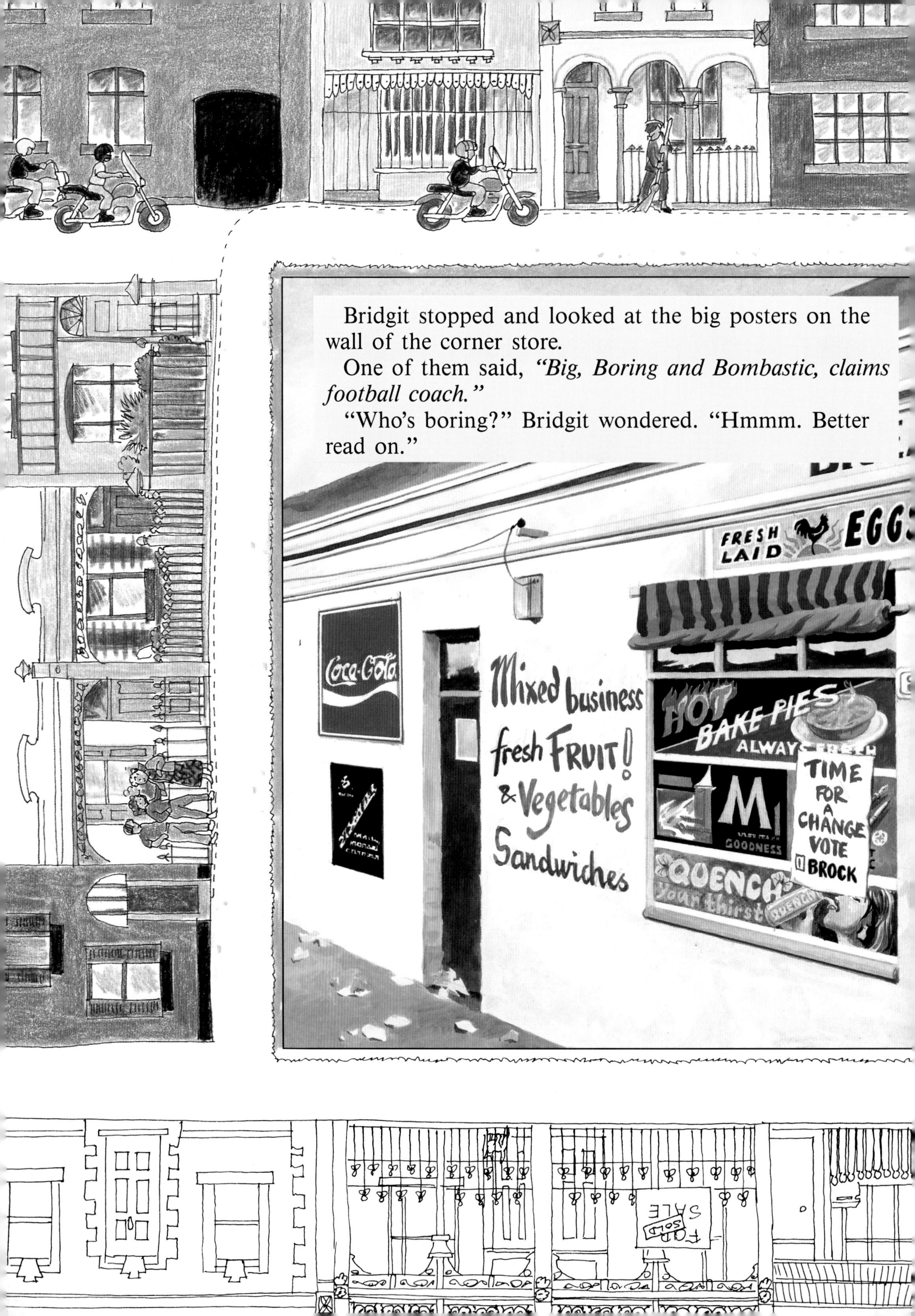

Bridgit stopped and looked at the big posters on the wall of the corner store.

One of them said, *"Big, Boring and Bombastic, claims football coach."*

"Who's boring?" Bridgit wondered. "Hmmm. Better read on."

BREAD MILK
MILK
NEWSPAPERS
HAR
CORNER
MAGAZINES
HAROLD'S
CORNER STORE
Streets
ice cream
NEW
FROM
SPLASH
SLIM
THE NEWS
BIG
BORING
AND
MBASTIC
CLAIMS
FOOTBALL
OPEN
milk

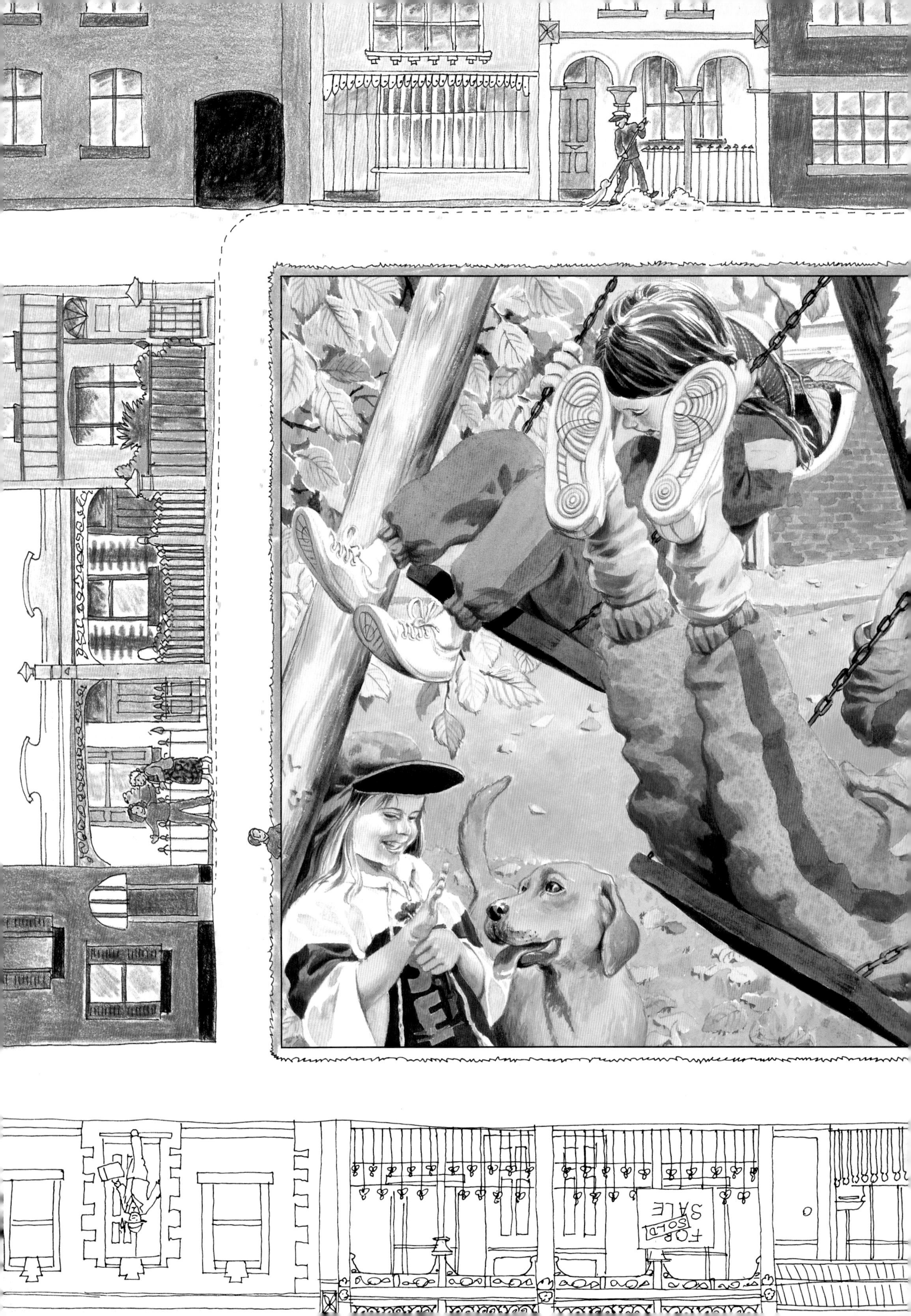
FOR SALE
SOLD

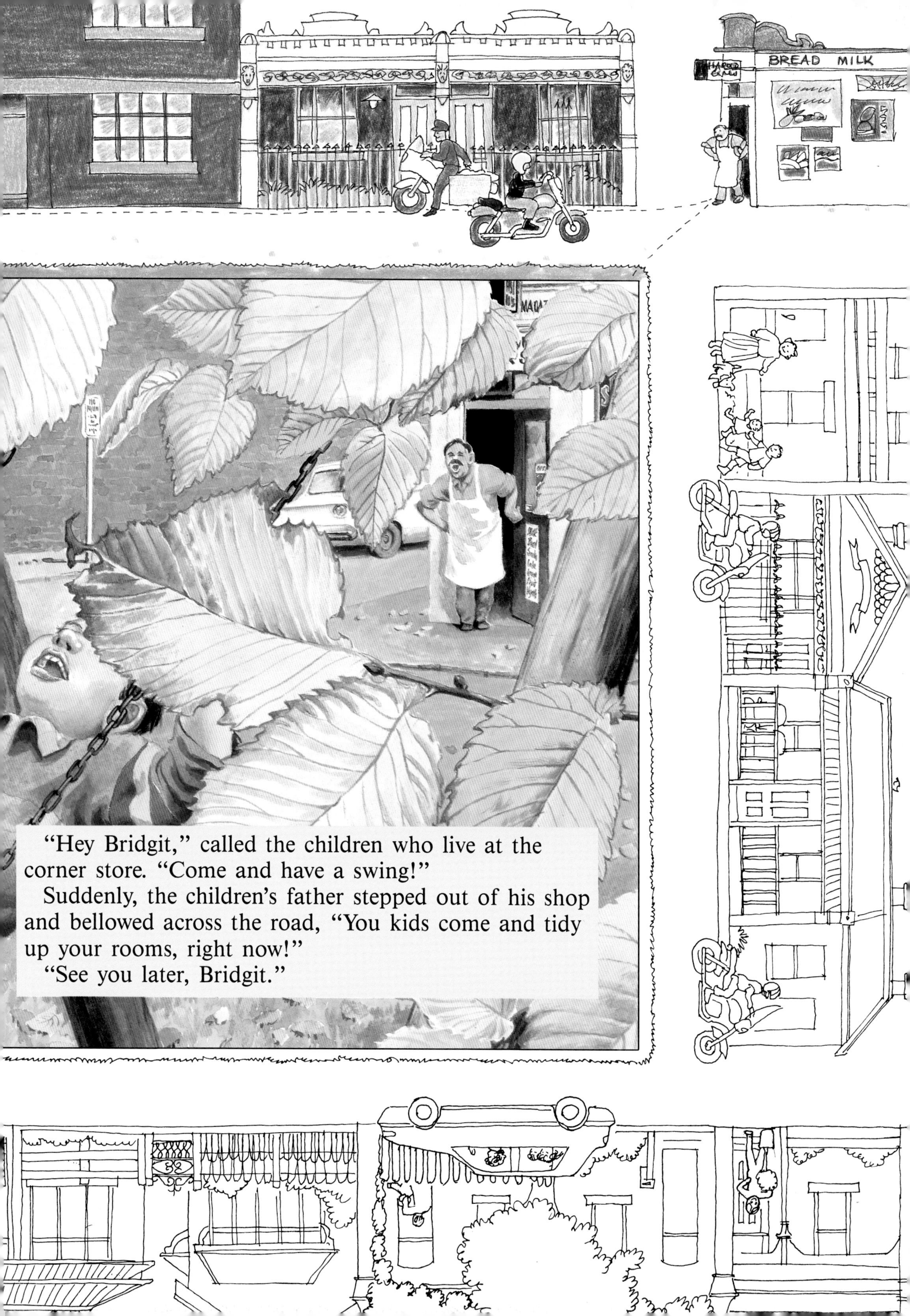

"Hey Bridgit," called the children who live at the corner store. "Come and have a swing!"

Suddenly, the children's father stepped out of his shop and bellowed across the road, "You kids come and tidy up your rooms, right now!"

"See you later, Bridgit."

FOR SALE
SOLD

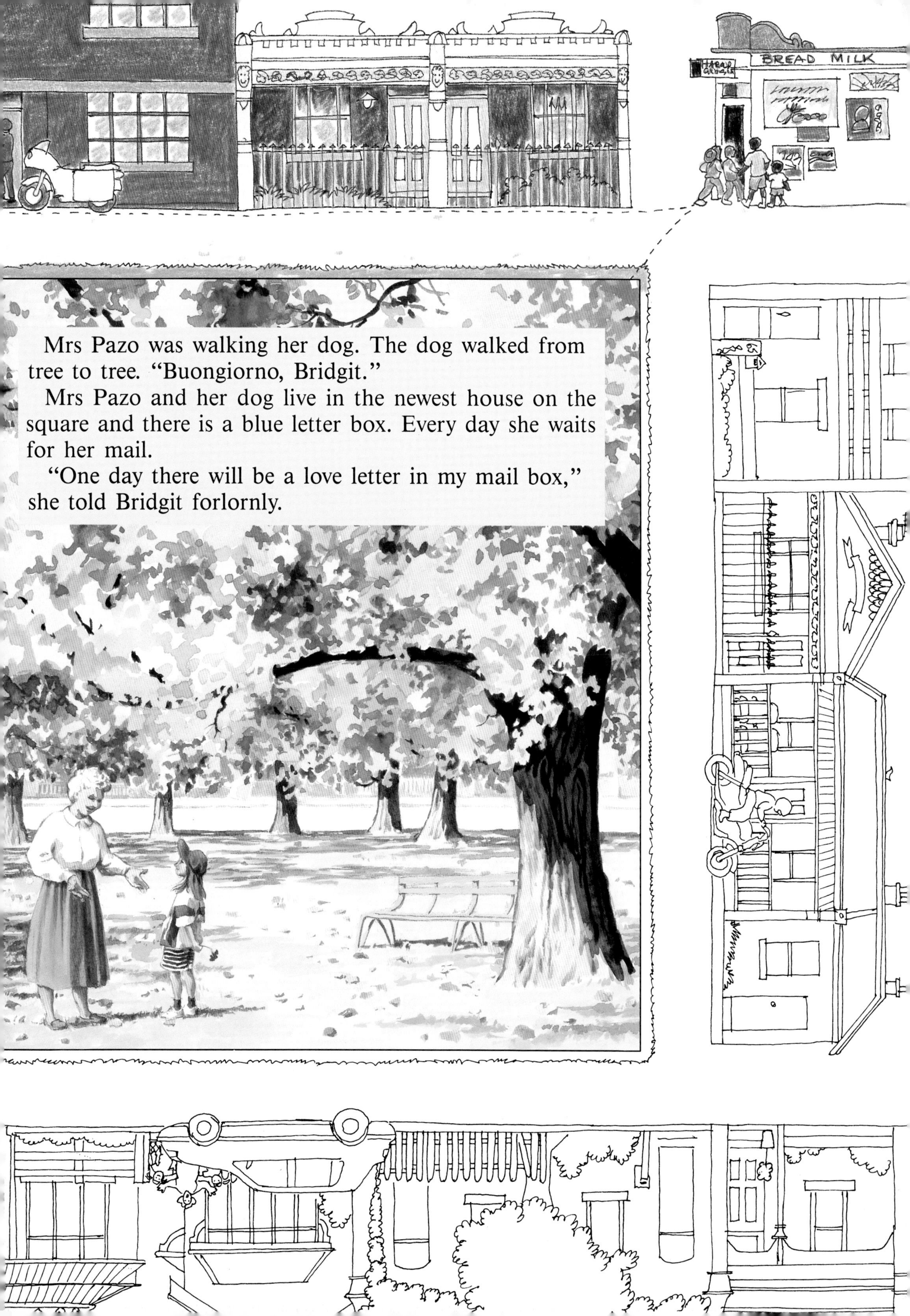

Mrs Pazo was walking her dog. The dog walked from tree to tree. "Buongiorno, Bridgit."

Mrs Pazo and her dog live in the newest house on the square and there is a blue letter box. Every day she waits for her mail.

"One day there will be a love letter in my mail box," she told Bridgit forlornly.

65
FOR SALE
SOLD

Bridgit left her red flower in Mrs Pazo's letter box. . . tee hee. . . and ran off.

Near Mrs Pazo's letter box were three pimply faced bikies called Roger, Dodger and Davis who were working on their machines.

"Gidday, Bridgit. Does your father have a torque wrench with a three-eighth socket and a wobbler extension?"

"Definitely not," said Bridgit, who wasn't sure what a torque wrench was.

BREAD MILK
HAROLD

RICH
REMOVALS
COUNTRY WIDE

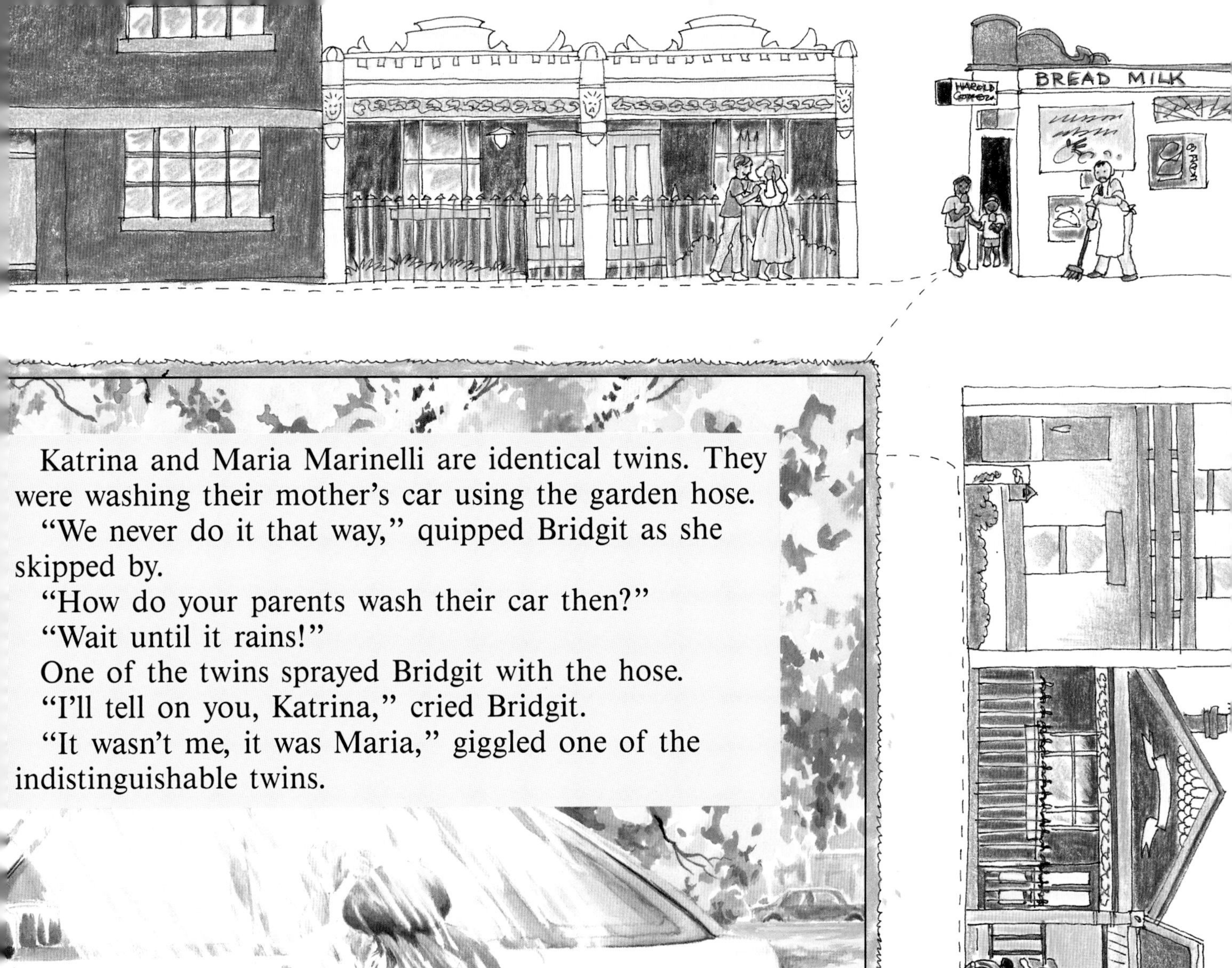

Katrina and Maria Marinelli are identical twins. They were washing their mother's car using the garden hose.

"We never do it that way," quipped Bridgit as she skipped by.

"How do your parents wash their car then?"

"Wait until it rains!"

One of the twins sprayed Bridgit with the hose.

"I'll tell on you, Katrina," cried Bridgit.

"It wasn't me, it was Maria," giggled one of the indistinguishable twins.

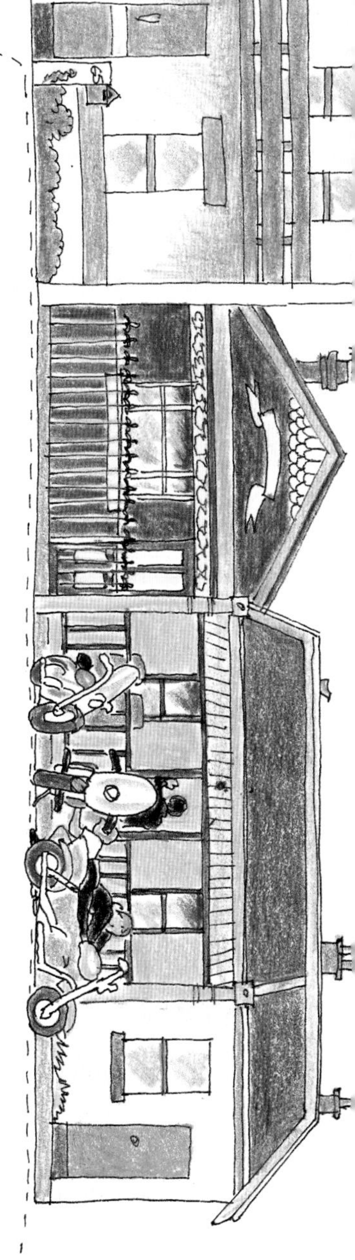

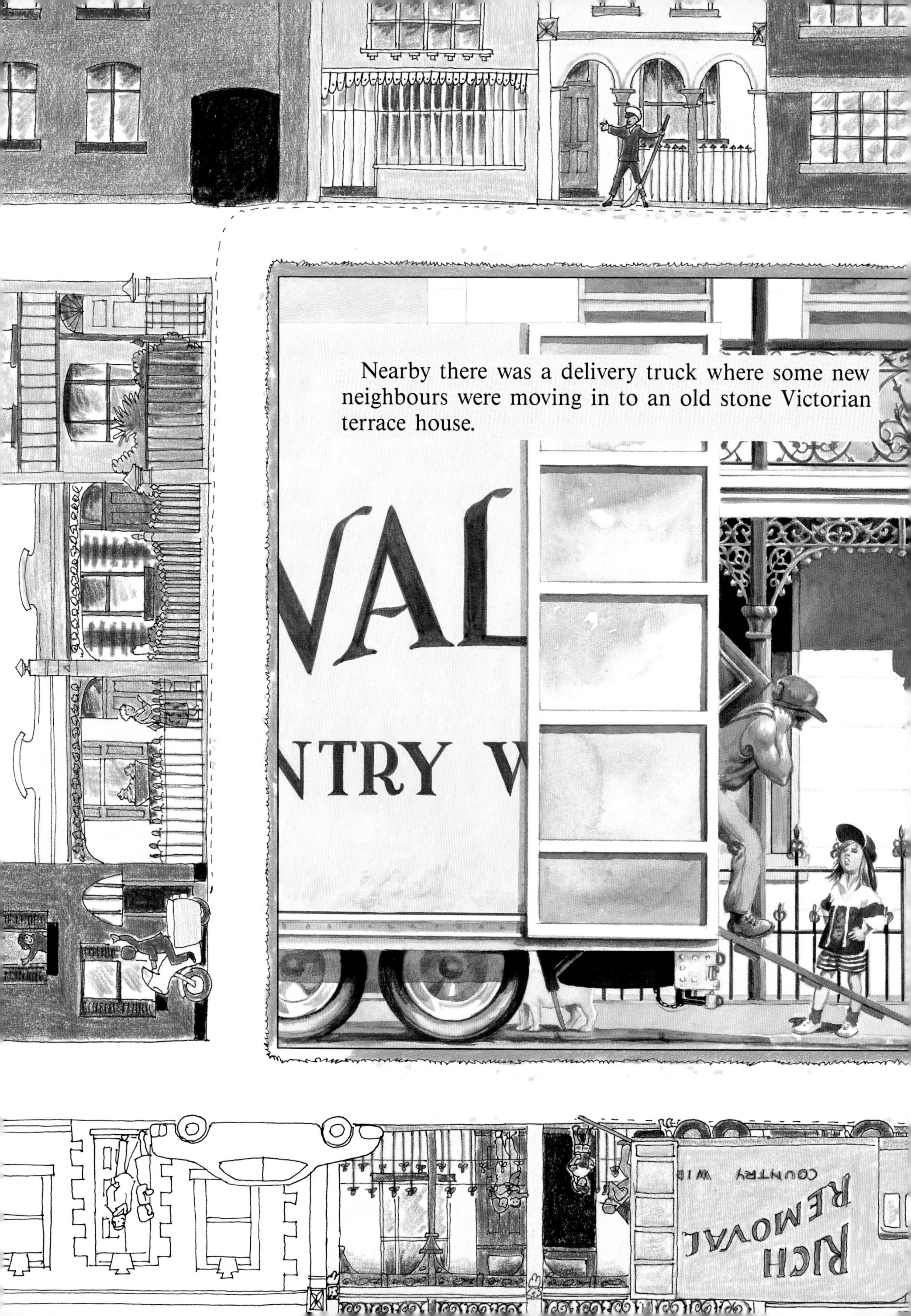

Nearby there was a delivery truck where some new neighbours were moving in to an old stone Victorian terrace house.

BREAD MILK

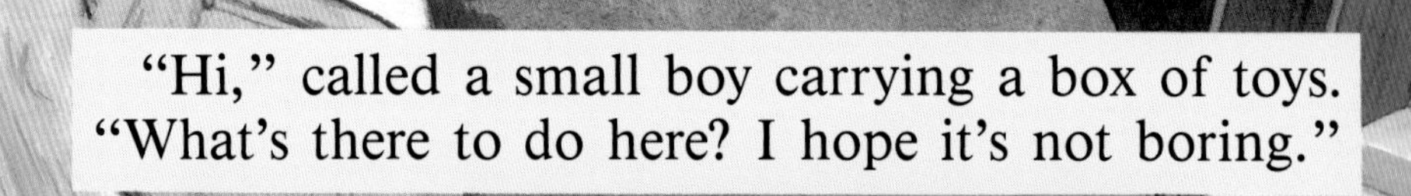

"Hi," called a small boy carrying a box of toys. "What's there to do here? I hope it's not boring."

BREAD MILK

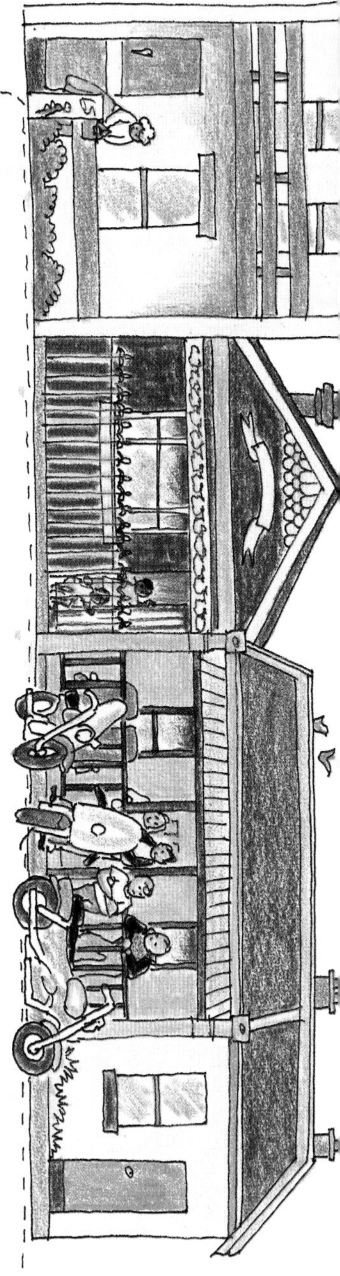

"No way! Come with me!"